Access your Online Resources

Mindy and Mo's Troll Trouble is accompanied by some downloadable material to help children practise the 't' sound.

Go to https://resourcecentre.routledge.com/speechmark and click on the cover of this book.

Answer the question prompt using your copy of the book to gain access to the online content.

T0284184

Mindy and Mo's Troll Trouble

Mindy and Mo love to play in a wood not far away. Join these two fun-loving adventurers as they get a lift from Titan the dragon to the wooded valley of the Tootles. Can Mindy and Mo help the Tootles make friends with Tub the troll before it's time to leave? What will the fallen tree be the next time they visit? And what will they see?

This Mindy and Mo story has been written to support children who are working on the 't' sound. Support your child's practise of their target sound by sharing Mindy and Mo's adventure in Tootle Valley and encouraging them to join in with the 'tub troll, tub troll' chant. Engaging characters and plot, supported by a rhythmic and rhyming structure, ensure this book not only supports speech development, but also entertains and inspires. Creatively and descriptively told, this story introduces new words and provides opportunities for developing literacy skills. Through positive characterisation, it also explores the themes of growth mindset, empathy, kindness and resilience, allowing children to make connections to their own lives and experiences.

A helpful section of suggested activities at the back of the book can be used to support further practise of the target speech sound. It also includes ideas for how this story can be used to help children to connect to nature through imagination. This humorous and triumphant story has been designed to support the individual child but is one which every child can enjoy!

Emily Kempster is an English teacher with 20 years' experience working in Gloucestershire secondary schools. Her passion for books inspired her to write from a young age, anything from short plays to ghost stories. More recently, in an attempt to entertain her young family and support her youngest daughter's difficulties with some speech sounds, she has focused on writing narrative poems. She hopes that the Mindy and Mo adventures will capture the imagination of young readers as well as support their speech sound development.

Lucy Cannon is a painter, illustrator and designer. Interested in all things creative from an early age, she studied Art and Graphic Design at college before heading into a successful management career in the voluntary sector. To follow her passion for art she set up Imagination by Lucy, which offers mural painting, illustration and creating custom home furnishings and apparel. Lucy is also involved in charity work, helping families who have children with heart conditions, but her most rewarding role to date is that of mum to two young children, one of whom had significant speech difficulties up to the age of 5. She now juggles time between bringing up her family, running her business, helping others and eating too much chocolate.

Rebecca Skinner is Head of Speech and Language Therapy and author at Thriving Language Community Interest Company. Co-founded by Rebecca and Becky Poulter Jewson, Thriving Language specialises in early years consultancy, offering training to early years settings and guest lecturing at universities on their undergraduate courses in Early Childhood Studies. Rebecca also works for the Gloucestershire Health and Care NHS Foundation Trust as a Specialist Speech and Language Therapist, specialising in early years and cleft palate.

Mindy and Mo's Troll Trouble

Emily Kempster, Lucy Cannon and Rebecca Skinner

Routledge
Taylor & Francis Group

LONDON AND NEW YORK

Designed cover image: Lucy Cannon

First published 2025
by Routledge
4 Park Square, Milton Park, Abingdon, Oxon OX14 4RN

and by Routledge
605 Third Avenue, New York, NY 10158

Routledge is an imprint of the Taylor & Francis Group, an informa business

© 2025 Emily Kempster, Lucy Cannon and Rebecca Skinner

The right of Emily Kempster and Rebecca Skinner to be identified as authors and Lucy Cannon to be identified as illustrator of this work has been asserted in accordance with sections 77 and 78 of the Copyright, Designs and Patents Act 1988.

British Library Cataloguing-in-Publication Data
A catalogue record for this book is available from the British Library

Library of Congress Cataloging-in-Publication Data
A catalog record has been requested for this book

ISBN: 978-1-032-86070-1 (pbk)
ISBN: 978-1-003-52125-9 (ebk)

DOI: 10.4324/9781003521259

This book can also be purchased as part of a set:
The Adventures of Mindy and Mo
ISBN: 978-1-032-43693-7 (pbk set)

Typeset in Futura Std
by Deanta Global Publishing Services, Chennai, India

Access the Support Material: https://resourcecentre.routledge.com/speechmark

Contents

Guidance for the Reader

We really hope you enjoy this Mindy and Mo adventure. There are seven others for you to read.

This series has been created by Rebecca Skinner, Specialist Speech and Language Therapist, Emily Kempster and Lucy Cannon in order to promote listening and awareness of specific speech sounds.

This book is loaded with the target sound 't', giving the reader opportunities to model this sound naturally to children.

Each Mindy and Mo story includes a fun chorus containing 'nonsense words'. Not knowing these words or having a pre-existing way of saying them, makes it easier for children to practise blending their 'tricky sound' into a word structure. Children may like to join you in saying the chorus as they become familiar with the story.

Sharing this book with children who are having difficulty with the sound 't' is a non-direct intervention, enabling you to support speech sound development in a fun way, without putting any pressure on the child.

These stories can be enjoyed by **all** children, enabling speech sound intervention to be fully inclusive.

Top tips

- Enjoy the story – children love to engage with stories and characters. This book can be enjoyed by all children.

- Talk naturally – you don't need to emphasise the target sound.

- Re-visit the story – you can raise the child's awareness of the target sound, for example 'tub troll' – "that starts with a 't'" (remember that we are talking about the sound 't' and not the letter 'tuh' or 'tee').

- Draw the child's attention to your mouth when you are talking about the target sound – "look at my mouth when I say 't', my tongue is tapping behind my teeth".

- Extend the experience – support children to use the ideas in the story to develop their imagination and vocabulary. When you are outside you might find a fallen tree or a 'magic tree' – where would you and your children like to go on your adventure?

Meet the Characters

 Hi, I'm Mindy! I'm pleased you're coming on an adventure with me and my friend Mo. We love playing outside, especially at the fallen tree – it's our favourite place. How the tree came to fall down, we don't know, but we do know that in our imagination we can turn it into whatever we like. Come on! Let's see where it takes us.

 Hi, I'm Mo – that's short for Morris. I love playing outside with Mindy at the fallen tree, it's always lots of fun. Sometimes I struggle to hear everything clearly, but my hearing aid helps with that. Outside noises are different to inside ones, I like them. Being outside helps me to hear better, especially when Mindy talks to me. I'm pleased you're coming to see the magical tree with us. Come on, let's explore.

 Don't forget me! I'm Sid the snail and I go on every adventure. See if you can spot me along the way.

Mindy and Mo love to play
In a wood not far away.
They head straight for the fallen tree.
What will it be? What will they see?

A dragon!

'Hold on tightly!' Mindy calls,
As Titan gives a mighty roar.
Over crashing waves below,
On past mountains topped with snow.

Determined Titan flies at speed,
The timid Tootles are in need.
'Tootle Valley's just in sight.
I hear the trumpet loud and bright!'

'Tub troll, tub troll, Tootles watch ou[t]
She tibs and she tobs and she tubs all about.'

Into the valley, Titan swoops,
The Tootles huddle in a group.
'Hi, friends, what's the trouble here?
We heard your trumpet, what's to fear?'

' Tub troll, tub troll, Tootles watch out!
She tibs and she tobs and she tubs all about.'

'The troll's been here, she took our book.
She dropped those Tolly flowers – look!
They only grow next to her cave
In Toto Wood, so grim and grave.'

'Our treasured book's a tub troll guide,
With how to keep us safe inside.'
'Then fly with us to Toto Wood,
We'll find your book. All will be good.'

'Tub troll, tub troll, Tootles watch out!
he tibs and She tobs and She tubs all about.'

Over twisty, rushing streams,
On past tree tops tall and green.
'Toto Wood, we're nearly there.
Don't worry, Tootle. Don't be scared.'

In Toto Wood it's dark and cold,
Yet Tolly flowers shine like gold.
'In here, I hear a troubled moan,
Someone's upset and all alone.'

Into a gloomy cave they walk,
'Hello there, would you like to talk?'
Lit by her lantern's gentle glow,
Sits one gigantic, lonely troll.

She lifts her head with tear-filled eyes
And seems so small despite her size.
Upturned snout and pointy teeth,
But soft and thoughtful underneath.

'I brought the Tolly flowers in peace,
Then read your book and dared not speak.
"How to Spot and Stop and Catch,
How to Set a Tub Troll Trap"....'

Regretting what they thought before,
The Tootle joins her on the floor.
'I'm sorry we've caused hurt and pain,
Come back with us, we must explain.'

To Tootle Valley Titan flies,
But now the team's a mighty five.
They swiftly land, the truth is told,
The Tootles meet the *real* tub troll.

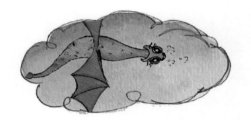

Tub troll, tub troll, Tootles' new friend,
Friendship and kindness must never end.'

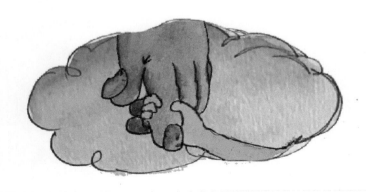

'Thank you, Mindy, thank you, Mo.
That we're now friends is down to you.'
'You feared the troll, her startling looks,
But all the cruelty was that book's.'

Mo and Mindy shout goodbye,
As Titan soars into the sky.
Over tumbling waterfalls,
On past ancient castle walls.

Mindy and Mo love to play
In a wood not far away.
Next time they visit the fallen tree,
What will it be? What will they see?

Further Activities: 't'

We hope you enjoyed sharing in the adventures of Mindy and Mo. The aim of this book is to entertain children with a fun story which is loaded with the target sound 't', providing them with opportunities to hear the sound and have a go.

Here are some further activities to support development of the sound 't'.

How do we produce the sound 't'?

The sound 't' is a quiet sound. It is produced by lifting the tongue tip up behind the top teeth, pushing it hard against the roof of the mouth to create pressure and then releasing this to allow the sound to burst through the mouth.

Ways you can promote the target sound 't'

- **Go on a sound hunt**
  Look around your environment for objects which start with a 't' (tap), have a 't' in the middle (letter) or a 't' at the end of the word (hat). Remember we are talking about the sound and not the letter. As you find your objects, talk about them together to raise your child's awareness of the sound 't' in the word.

- **Find the 't'**
  Gather a pile of objects or pictures, some of which start with the sound 't' and others starting with different sounds. Together find all the items which start with a 't'. Select one item at a time, say the word and think aloud: does it start with a 't'? If the child is struggling to say the sound 't' accurately, say the word to them so they can hear the sound modelled.

- **Hide and seek**
  Collect pictures of objects that start with a 't', have a 't' in the middle or a 't' at the end of the word. Take turns to hide the pictures in different places in your environment while the other person closes their eyes. Name the pictures as you find them. Remember you will need to model the words if the child is struggling to say the sound 't'.

Important

These activities should be fun, so please remember not to put pressure on the child to say the sound. Enjoy the book and use the activities to model the target sound and support speech sound development.

More ways in which this book can be enjoyed and encourage your child to imagine, explore and learn

1. Head outside and find a tree. Use your imagination: What could the tree become? Where could it take you? What could you see and do there?

2. What does a tree need to grow? How does a tree change each season? How do trees feel when you touch them?

3. The tub troll feels sad because the Tootles don't include her. Can you think of a time when someone included you in a game?

Word List

Words starting with 't'	Words with 't' in the middle	Words ending with 't'
Tap	Letter	Hat
Tea	Writing	Mat
Ten	Party	Net
Top	Water	Wet
Toe	Potty	Goat
Teeth	Button	Sit